Very Best Friend

Written by Robina Beckles Willson

Illustrated by Stella Voce

Chapter 1
A Secret Power

'Leave some for me,' said a tiny voice.

Ted looked round, but there was no one in sight. He thought he must have been dreaming. He took another bite of his biscuit and tried to find a more comfortable position on the hard back door step.

'And don't squash me either,' said the voice.

'Where are you? Who are you?' asked Ted.

'No need to shout. I can hear you perfectly well.'

'But I can't see you at all,' said Ted. He wondered who might appear at any moment.

'We can't all be giants,' the voice told him.

'Do you mean me?' asked Ted. 'But I'm not a giant. I'm quite small. Some of the boys at school are much taller.'

'And are they selfish with their biscuits too?' the voice went on.

'Well,' said Ted, 'if you want some of mine, you'd better show yourself. It's nearly all gone.' As Ted spoke, a field mouse with a long tail darted out from a tiny hole under the door step.

'You put out food for the birds,' she said. 'But never a crumb for me.'

'I didn't even know you lived here,' said Ted.

'Well now you know, so how about a bit of biscuit?'

Ted put some crumbs on the ground, and watched the mouse eat them, her whiskers flicking.

Suddenly Ted realised that he had understood all the mouse had said. And the mouse had understood him too. Ted knew he wasn't dreaming now.

'Do you talk to other people?' Ted asked.

'Oh no,' the mouse replied. 'They wouldn't listen.'

Ted felt dazed. He had stumbled on a secret power, and although he liked mice, his mum said they were into everything, especially food. So he knew she would not welcome a mouse in the house.

'I've got to go now. I'll come and see you again,' he said.

'I'll look out for you. And save me a bit more biscuit next time,' said the mouse, as she scuttled out of sight.

'I wonder if I can talk to other animals?' Ted thought, as he walked down the small garden which he and his mum shared with Mr Appleby who lived in the flat upstairs. At the bottom of the garden was an old ash tree, which Ted often climbed. His neighbour's two cats were there, sharpening their claws on the tree trunk.

'Hello cats,' he said shyly.

'Oh, so you've decided to speak to us after all this time, have you?' said one cat. 'And what is your name?'

'Ted.'

'Rather a small name. I suppose it's the best you could manage. I am called Arabella, and my sister is Henrietta.'

'Pleased to meet you,' said the other cat. 'You like cats, do you?'

'Yes, I've often seen you climbing up and down the trees. I wish I could get as high.'

'The lady who lives with us never climbs the trees in our garden,' said Henrietta.

'My mum doesn't either,' said Ted. 'So you won't meet her up here. She isn't as keen on cats as I am,' he added. He thought he had better make sure they didn't come to his back door. They might find the mouse hole there.

'But how can your mum dislike cats, when we're such beautiful creatures?' asked Arabella.

'And so good at hunting,' remarked her sister. 'I could catch any bird in this garden if I wanted to.'

'But aren't you fed at home? Doesn't your owner give you cat food and milk?' asked Ted, feeling sorry for the birds.

'Yes, we have everything we could wish. I just love chasing and catching them,' said Henrietta.

'Don't worry,' added Arabella. 'She usually misses, and the birds laugh all the way up to the sky.'

The next day, on his way to school, Ted saw a flock of pigeons near the park. They flew down and began to talk to him.

'What's in your bag?' they demanded.

'My packed lunch,' Ted answered.

'You don't need all that, do you?' said the biggest speckled pigeon, peck-pecking at the ground.

'I do,' said Ted. 'I'm hungry by break-time at school, and I start some of my lunch then. If I gave it to all of you, I'd starve. Anyway, I must be off or I'll be late for school.'

'What do you do in school?' asked the white pigeon.

'Oh, we learn things,' said Ted.

'Like finding food? Or flying?' asked the speckled pigeon.

'No, they don't teach us flying at school,' Ted told her. 'I think I'm made for walking and running.'

'Poor you,' said the pigeon. 'What a dull life, stuck to the ground. Come on, everyone.'

They rose, flapping in the air. Ted wished that he could fly to school or even better, not go to school at all, but fly off somewhere exciting.

Ted soon noticed that if he met any of his friends on the way to school none of the creatures spoke to him. So he kept his secret to himself. Anyway, Ted knew that no one would believe that animals talked to him when he was on his own, although there was one animal that wouldn't talk to him.

At the corner of Ted's road was a run-down house, where a big shaggy dog lived. Sometimes he stood still in the front window, but more often than not he was tied up in the garden by the front door. And although Ted waved and smiled and said 'Hello', the dog did not even look at him. He stared into the distance with his mouth shut tight. Perhaps he was proud. Perhaps he was unhappy.

Ted was puzzled.

What animals talked to Ted?
Why do you think the dog wouldn't talk to Ted?

Chapter 2
A Dog in Distress

So that afternoon, Ted consulted Mouse. 'Since I've met you, all the other creatures I've seen have spoken to me. I wonder why the dog at the corner won't say a word?'

'Don't ask me. Maybe he's bad-tempered, or doesn't like boys. Perhaps he's scared of you.'

'I don't think it's that,' said Ted. 'I'm sure there's something wrong with him. I'm going to try and talk to him again. Would you like to come?'

Mouse hesitated. 'He is rather a big dog, you say?'

'I'll look after you,' said Ted. 'You could go in my pocket. I'd like to know what you think.'

'All right. I'll just shut up my house,' said Mouse.

Mouse rolled a pebble over her mouse hole, then allowed Ted to pick her up and put her in his pocket.

When they reached the corner house Mouse asked, 'What's that written on the gate?'

'BEWARE OF THE DOG,' read Ted.

'Then he really is fierce,' said Mouse, ducking down inside Ted's pocket again.

'I'm going to see for myself,' said Ted, leaning over the front gate. The dog stood perfectly still, his head low.

Ted spoke softly. 'Hello, I've come to talk to you because I think you look lonely, standing by yourself every day. I haven't come to bother you, just to say hello.'

Mouse peeked out when there was no answer. The dog had not moved. His eyes were watery and he looked sad. It almost looked as if he was crying. The fur under his chin which looked like a beard, and his oval paws, should have been white, but they were dirty and matted. His fur grew in uneven tufts, as if he had never been brushed.

'Who sent you?' the dog asked huskily.

'No one. I came myself,' said Ted gently.

'Your voice is kind,' said the dog. 'I had forgotten that anyone could speak like that.'

'Why?' asked Ted.

'My master always shouts at me,' answered the dog. 'He says I don't guard his house well enough. I used to bark a lot, but now I'm too tired to care.'

'Does he feed you?' asked Ted.

'A bit, when he comes back. I never know when he's coming.'

'Does he take you out for walks?' Ted went on.

'No, he expects me to guard the house.'

'But there's a park at the end of the road,' said Ted.

'I've never been there,' the dog told Ted.

Ted looked shocked. 'But your master doesn't leave you out here all night, does he?'

'Sometimes. Then he comes home early in the morning, kicks me for not barking when he opens the gate, and goes inside and sleeps half the day. I don't often go inside the house now,' said the dog, sadly.

'He sounds cruel,' said Ted. 'I wish I could do something for you.' He opened the gate and put out his hand, wanting to stroke the dog. But the dog cowered away, growling in his throat.

'He *has* been bad to you,' said Ted

slowly, not touching him after all. 'I'll come and see you again.'

'Be careful if you do,' said the dog, 'because he might turn on you, if he catches you.'

Ted looked round the garden. He noticed that there was another gate in the side road, which might be useful if he needed to make a quick getaway.

'I will come back,' he promised, trying not to sound scared. Then Ted heard a sniffling sound coming from his pocket.

'What did you think of that, Mouse?'

'It's the saddest thing I've ever heard,' said Mouse. 'A great big dog like that treated so badly.'

Chapter 3
Why Not Let Him Go?

When he got home from school, Ted often went to see Mr Appleby, who lived upstairs. Today he decided to ask him about dogs.

Mr Appleby took down his old encyclopedia. It had pictures of all the different breeds of dogs.

Ted pointed to one. 'That's the dog I've been telling you about, the one down the road.'

'He's a bearded collie, a shepherding dog,' Mr Appleby read out, 'a very friendly breed. Needs regular exercise, and a lot of grooming to look after his long coat.'

'He has none of that,' said Ted, 'because he's cruelly treated and half-starved.'

'How do you know he's treated so cruelly?' said Mr Appleby.

'I just know,' Ted answered mysteriously. He couldn't tell Mr Appleby that the dog had told him. He wouldn't believe that. 'What can I do to help the poor dog?' asked Ted.

'You could report the owner to the RSPCA, the Royal Society for the Prevention of Cruelty to Animals.'

'Wouldn't it be easier if someone let the dog loose?' asked Ted.

'People can't go around doing that sort of thing,' said Mr Appleby. 'If a dog is being cruelly treated, I think the police would take it to a dogs' home. You could ask your mum.'

Ted thanked Mr Appleby and went out into the garden. The flock of pigeons were there, led by the biggest one called Speckles.

'So this is where all your big lunches are packed,' Speckles said. 'Is your house full of food then?'

Ted laughed. 'Not really.'

'Any left-overs?' Speckles asked hopefully.

'I'll go and see,' said Ted, and went indoors for a bit of bread.

When he came back a white pigeon was chirruping, 'Cats-cats-cats-cats-cats.'

'It's all right. These two cats are friends of *mine*,' said Ted. 'Stay up on the wall please, Arabella and Henrietta.'

Ted scattered breadcrumbs on the ground. The cats crept menacingly along the top of the wall, so the pigeons pecked at the crumbs quickly, and then flew off.

'They *have* to hunt for their food,' Ted told the cats, 'and now you've scared them away.'

'Don't worry. I wouldn't fancy a whole pigeon,' said Henrietta. 'I just like to see them fly away from our garden.'

'My garden,' Ted corrected her. 'I've found out about the dog down the road. He's got a horrible master, who kicks and hits him.'

'Why doesn't he bite him back?' asked Henrietta.

'I think the man must be too strong. And the dog's frightened of him,' said Ted.

'Then he should run away,' suggested Arabella.

'But where to? And don't forget he's tied up,' explained Ted.

'Then you must let him go. It's simple,' said Henrietta.

'I can't look after him properly. Dogs need lots of food. And somewhere to live.'

'But you can't leave him there, can you? He has to have a bit of help, like we do from our lady. That's what people are for,' said Arabella.

'I don't know what I can do,' said Ted.

Ted walked back towards the house to tell Mouse about his talk with Mr Appleby.

'That breed of dog should be very friendly, but he's scared of even a boy coming near him,' said Ted.

'I can understand that, when he's been tied up by that man,' said Mouse.

'You'll have to help him, Ted. You're like a brave giant to me,' said Mouse admiringly.

'You'll have to kidnap the dog,'
Mouse told him. 'Bring the dog here.
It's an enormous house.'

'It's Mr Appleby's house. We only
have the downstairs flat. And my mum
wouldn't let me have a dog. She says it's
not fair leaving him in all day, when
she's at work and I'm at school.'

'I can't think what you go to school
for,' said Mouse, 'when you could be
here playing in the garden.'

'I'm on holiday now. And I come
into the garden as often as I can, now
I've met you,' said Ted, stroking her
with one finger.

Mouse swelled a little with pleasure.

Ted started thinking about the dog again. 'I suppose I could take him to the police station, if only I dared,' Ted went on.

'You've got to do something,' Mouse told him. 'You're his only hope.'

Do you think Ted will try to rescue the dog?
If so, how would he do it?

Chapter 4
Rescue Plans

'I've decided!' Ted told Mouse the next day. 'I am going to try and kidnap the dog.'

'I knew you would,' said Mouse.

'There's a lot to plan,' said Ted. 'We have to warn the dog and I ought to have someone to be a look-out while I set him free, so the man doesn't catch me at it.'

'I'll stay with you, in case you need me to bite the man for you,' said Mouse. 'I wouldn't make a good look-out because I'm far too small.'

'Thank you, Mouse,' said Ted. 'I was thinking I could ask the cats to sit up the tree in the front garden, and yowl if they see him coming.'

'They would be well out of the way up there,' Mouse agreed promptly.

'We don't know what the man looks like yet, so we'll have to find out,' said Ted.

Mouse hid in Ted's pocket while Ted went up the garden to talk to the cats.

'I've decided to set that poor dog free,' he told them.

'Just as I suggested,' said Henrietta.

'But I will need you to keep watch,' Ted explained. 'Come along and I'll show you.'

So they went down the road, with the cats frisking in and out of the front gardens. At the corner, the dog was sitting near the front door as usual. When he saw Ted he said, 'Watch out! My master's back. If he sees I've let someone in the garden he'll go wild.'

'But we want to see what he looks like,' Ted explained. 'I'm planning to set you free, and I've asked my cat friends here to look out for him while I do it, in case your master turns up suddenly.'

'You really think you can set me free?' asked the dog.

'I'm going to try,' said Ted, kneeling down to inspect the thick rope which was fastened to a collar round the dog's neck. The collar's buckle looked as if it would be too stiff for his fingers. It would be easier to cut the rope.

'What does your master look like?'

'He's a big ugly man with black hair. And he has cruel eyes,' said the dog.

Ted shuddered. 'I'll run if he comes out.'

'Yes, you must!' said the dog.

The cats had arranged themselves in a tree nearby.

'Today, we'll just find out what he looks like,' said Ted.

'But he may stay indoors till dark,' the dog told them.

'I can't stay that long. My mum would be worried,' said Ted. 'How can we make him come out?'

'I know,' said Arabella. 'Henrietta and I could sing together. I have noticed that some people don't like our duets. So I think Henrietta's voice can't be as sweet as mine.'

'Nonsense,' said Henrietta. 'Listen to this, Ted.' She began to miaow. Arabella joined in, yelling and yowling.

It was an amazing sound. The dog stood open-mouthed.

Suddenly, the front door opened. Ted rushed out to the pavement and hid while a large man came out, shouting furiously.

'Can't you keep those caterwauling cats out of my garden, you good-for-nothing dog!'

He kicked the dog and bellowed at the cats. 'Get out of here, or I'll turn the hose on you!'

Then he picked up a dustbin lid and threw it at their tree. Ted watched in alarm, glad to be unseen as the cats arched their backs and hissed with rage.

The man went back into the house and slammed the door.

'What a horrible man,' said Arabella.

'Yes,' Henrietta agreed. 'And he obviously doesn't know good music when he hears it. I'd be pleased to help you set the dog free from such an ogre.'

'So would I,' added Arabella.

'Now at least we know what the man looks like,' said Ted. 'We'll come back tomorrow to set you free.'

Then they said goodbye to the dog, and as the cats chased each other over garden walls, Ted walked home with Mouse cupped in his hand.

'Arabella's right. He really is a horrible man,' said Ted.

'I think you will need more help than those moaning cats,' warned Mouse.

'But who?' asked Ted.

Then, as he spoke he noticed a flock of pigeons take off towards the park. 'Perhaps the pigeons could help us. If they perched on the roof, they could watch out for the man too.'

Ted went along to the park gates and spoke to Speckles, describing the dog's owner.

'You could look out while we get the dog safely away from his bad master. I'll buy you a bread roll,' he promised, 'and you can have it as soon as the dog is free.'

'Better make it two rolls,' Speckles told him, 'in case all the family wants to come on the outing.'

'It's a rescue operation, not an outing,' said Ted.

Chapter 5
Set Free for a While

The next morning, Ted bought two rolls, sent the cats ahead down the road and went to collect the pigeons from the park, with Mouse hiding in his pocket.

The pigeons were thrilled to be out in a flock, and swooped about Ted excitedly.

'Do tell them it's not a party,' Ted said to Speckles.

'They've heard about the free food afterwards,' Speckles explained.

Ted set off under the flapping wings. At the dog's house he found the two cats up in the tree.

'What do we need those birds for? They'd better keep their distance from me,' said Henrietta threateningly.

'The pigeons are going up on the roof,' Ted replied. 'Then, when they hear you say that the man is coming, they'll fly down and get in his way. That's if he turns up before I've finished the rescue.'

'He's out at the moment,' the dog told them. 'Hasn't been home all night.'

'Good,' said Ted, kneeling beside the dog and taking out his penknife. 'I'll start at once. Look out now everybody! As I can't get the collar undone, I think it's best to cut the rope,' he explained again to Mouse, who had crept out on to the ground, bravely risking being seen by the cats.

As Ted began to hack at the rope, a pigeon flew down and asked, 'Is it dinner-time yet?'

'No, it's not. And no bread for pigeons who don't keep watch,' Ted answered sharply.

'Keep very still,' he told the dog. 'It's a thick rope. And my penknife isn't very sharp.'

'I'll help with my teeth,' offered Mouse.

Suddenly there was a terrible noise, and Mouse nearly jumped back into Ted's pocket.

A car stopped outside the house, and the dog's owner opened the gate.

Both cats yowled loudly. The pigeons flew down and flapped around.

One perched on the man's head; two more clawed his shoulders. The man tried to make his way up the front path, beating them off with his thick arms, struggling to get his door key out of his pocket as they flocked round him.

Mouse chewed frantically. Ted used his fingers to tear apart the last threads of the rope. At last it broke in two. Ted scooped Mouse into his pocket, grabbed the loose end attached to the collar and shouted 'Run!' to the dog. They ducked out through the side gate before the man could think of stopping them.

Running as fast as they could, they rounded the corner and hurried down the road. Ted was too scared even to notice whether his bird friends were with him or not.

He ran straight to the police station. The pigeons were already there, clustering on the step.

'Reward, Ted,' they murmured. 'We've come for the bread, remember. Quickly, before our town cousins, who are a greedy gang, find us and want a share.'

Ted pulled the two squashed rolls out of his pocket, and crumbled them up. 'Thank you, pigeons, for all your help. I'll give you some more another day.'

They were too busy pecking to answer. Ted patted the dog reassuringly, went into the police station and walked up to a high counter.

A policeman looked down from the other side and asked, 'And what can we do for you, young man?'

'I've come to bring you this dog. His owner has been cruel to him.'

'Oh has he now? Let's have a look at the both of you.'

The policeman lifted a flap and came round to Ted's side of the counter, then led them to a small room, where he sat at a table and took out a pen and pad.

'Sit you down and let's hear your story,' said the policeman.

Ted was glad to sit down, as suddenly his legs were wobbly. He kept his hand on the dog as he tried to answer the policeman's questions.

'How do you know he's been cruelly treated then?' asked the policeman.

'I just know,' said Ted. 'Look at the state of him.'

'He could certainly do with a bit more care, and that's what we'll suggest to his master. Poor old thing has been neglected a bit,' said the policeman.

'He's been neglected a lot,' said Ted.

'Leave it to us, son, and we'll look into it. You can't just help yourself to a dog, you know,' the policeman went on.

'I rescued him,' said Ted.

'I expect it felt like that,' said the policeman kindly. 'And it's good to see a boy bothering about animals, but he must go back to his owner.'

Ted couldn't think of anything else to say. The policeman took his name and address and told him to go straight home.

Ted could hardly bear to look at the
dog. He went to give him a pat, to say
goodbye, but the dog just cowered
away. Ted went home feeling he had
let him down.

When Ted got home his mother was cross. 'Where have you been? I've been so worried,' she said.

Ted said as little as he could while she told him off, then he went out into the garden.

When Mouse and the cats heard what had happened at the police station, they were very disappointed.

'I wish we'd hidden the dog here,' said Mouse.

'He's a bit big for that!' said Ted.

Then Henrietta spoke up. 'You mean you let them take him back to that ogre, after all our trouble?'

'I couldn't stop them,' Ted said sadly.

When Speckles flew by, Ted had to tell him the rest of the story too. Each time Ted described what had happened at the police station he felt worse, because he had not been able to help the poor dog.

Then a little later that day, Speckles called back to see Ted.

'I have exciting news,' he squawked. 'The police have kidnapped your dog.'

'How? What do you mean?' asked
Ted.

'Well, two policemen took the dog
back to his old house and they went
inside. After a while, they came out
again and they brought the dog out
with them.'

'By himself?'

'No, with the man.'

Ted was anxious to hear more, but
before he could get any more
information from Speckles he heard his
mother calling.

'Ted, come in at once, there's a policeman to see you.'

'What's the matter?' asked Ted, as he went into the kitchen.

'No need to look worried, Ted,' said the policeman he had met earlier. 'I've just come round to put you and your mum in the picture. When we took the dog back, we wanted to have a word with his owner. It's not fair to treat a dog as he did. And guess what we found? He had loads of stolen goods there – clocks, jewellery, videos and cameras. So we've taken him in for questioning.'

'He's a burglar then,' said Mum.

'That's what it looks like, madam,' said the policeman.

'But what about the dog?' asked Ted. 'Who'll look after him?'

'He'll be fine. We're taking him to the dogs' home. They'll look after the dog while we sort things out. His owner says he never wants to see him again. And the dog will be better off there, thanks to this young man.'

'You should have told me about all this, Ted, and not just taken the dog, however badly he'd been treated,' said Mum. 'I can understand how you felt but you should be pleased that he's safe now.'

But somehow Ted didn't feel pleased, only flat.

Why do you think Ted doesn't feel pleased?

Chapter 6

At the Dogs' Home

'I'm sure the dog is being looked after, but I would like to see him again,' Ted admitted to Mouse the next day.

'Then why don't you go and visit him at the dogs' home?' Mouse asked. 'I want to know how he is too. I helped to set him free, don't forget.'

'You certainly did. I'll ask my mum about it.'

Ted's mum phoned the dogs' home from Mr Appleby's flat, while he and Ted listened.

'I see. 50p for adults and 20p for children to see the dogs,' she said. 'And you're open all day Saturday. Yes, I'll be with my son. Thank you very much.'

'If we go, it might be quite sad to see all those unwanted dogs,' she warned Ted.

'I'd just like to see the dog we rescued,' he said.

'They're well looked after, so you'll see an improvement,' Mr Appleby told him. 'And when they're fit, they're sent to new homes.'

'Can we go soon?' urged Ted.

'All right, this Saturday,' his mum promised.

Ted could hear the dogs barking and yapping as he and his mum came near the dogs' home.

A keeper wearing a dogs' home T-shirt and jeans and a bunch of keys on a chain came up to them and asked, 'Are you looking for the dogs for sale?'

'No, thank you, we're looking for a dog who came here a few days ago,' answered Mum.

'He's a bearded collie,' added Ted.

'Oh, we call him Beardie. He's quite a live wire. Had a rough time before we took him in. He's down this row and across the yard. Ask again if you get lost.'

'This place is much bigger than I
thought it would be,' said Ted as they
walked along rows and rows of cages of
dogs. At last Ted saw a bearded collie in a
cage by himself. He hurried over to him.

As soon as the dog saw Ted he rushed round and round in his cage, then tried to put out a paw, panting with delight.

Ted was wondering how they could talk to each other, but luckily, just then his mum said, 'I'll go and have a look at the other dogs if you want to stay with him for a while. He looks different from when he was down our road.'

Ted sat on the ground as near to the cage as possible, offering his fingers for Beardie to lick.

'Is it all right here?' he asked at once. 'They do look after you?'

'Oh yes, and there's plenty to eat. It's boring, that's all. I can't play with the other dogs, and when we have exercise it's just quick walks with the keepers. Some of the dogs cry a lot too, which I don't like. I'm not crying for my old master!'

'You'll never go back to him,' said Ted. 'My mum says he might go to prison, now they've caught him stealing things.'

'Some pigeons told me he'd stayed at the police station,' said Beardie.

'Are they the park pigeons who helped when we rescued you?' asked Ted.

'No, I think they're cousins,' said Beardie, 'but they'd heard all about my escape, because Speckles often flies over to town. The best pigeon here is called Dora. She comes round for any scraps in the cages and brings me the news.'

Ted didn't want to leave Beardie shut in his cage, but he had a good idea. 'Why don't we send messages to each other by pigeon?'

'I'd like that,' said Beardie. 'It would help a bit. Now I'm well again I wish I could go for a run with you in that park near your house. All I can do here is jump up and down.'

He started to show Ted how high he could go, but a keeper came by and said, 'Now calm down, Beardie. You'll be getting the other dogs worked up, and we don't want that, do we?'

'See what I mean,' muttered Beardie.

'My mum's coming back,' said Ted. 'I'll have to go. I didn't dare bring the mouse who bit your rope for me, but she sent you her love.'

After that, Dora the town pigeon, called to see Ted every day.

'I've heard the rescue story from Beardie and my cousin Speckles,' she told Ted. 'Those park pigeons seem to think they did it all.'

'They were a great help,' said Ted. 'But there were two cats and a mouse as well as them and me.'

'It must have been exciting,' said Dora.

'It was pretty scary too. How's Beardie today?' asked Ted.

'He's fine. One of the keepers was calling him "Gutsy", because he's so hungry,' said Dora.

'He was half-starved before,' Ted told her. 'So he must enjoy having plenty of food.'

'I feel the same myself,' said Dora, looking at Ted with orange eyes. 'It's a long fly from the dogs' home to your house.'

'I'll get you a snack,' Ted said, and he found a broken biscuit in the tin.

'He'll take a lot of feeding, that dog of yours,' said Dora.

'He's not mine. I wish he were,' said Ted longingly.

'Oh, by the way, they've put him with the "For Sale" dogs,' said Dora. 'Did I tell you that?'

'No, you didn't,' said Ted. 'Now I'll probably never see Beardie again.'

Chapter 7
A Tremendous Surprise

That afternoon, Ted found the cats prowling around his house. They thought they had earned a reward.

'If we hadn't sounded the alarm, that man would have caught you and shut you in his house,' Henrietta hinted.

'You were both marvellous,' said Ted quickly. 'I've been wondering what to give you as a present.'

'We do like fish, but don't trouble yourself,' said Henrietta airily.

'I'm not sure about fish, but I could probably manage a saucer of milk,' said Ted.

Just then Ted heard the sound of beating wings. He went to the gate and saw a whole flock of pigeons flying low.

'Oh, no! Dora's brought her family. I'll never have enough food for them all,' thought Ted.

Then he noticed that a dog
was running along the pavement. The
pigeons hovered in the air above the dog.
Ted nearly stopped breathing with
surprise, because the dog was Beardie.
As they reached him, Ted rushed to hug
Beardie.

'What? How? Why?' He tried to ask all
at once, while Dora landed beside him.

'We've brought Beardie for you to
have, Ted. He was so fed up with the
dogs' home, I thought he should come
and live with you.'

'But I can't…' gasped Ted.

'Well, we had a hard job getting him here, so you'll *have* to take him,' said Dora.

'Come in and tell me all about it,' said Ted.

The other pigeons nid-nodded as they walked round the front garden while Dora explained, 'When Beardie's keeper came to open the "For Sale" cage to take him for a walk, me and my friends flew round and round her head. She got in a muddle and Beardie slipped out of the cage.'

'So fast, no one could catch me,' added Beardie.

'They were too surprised. You should have seen him jumping over a wall!' said Dora excitedly. 'And we town pigeons led him here all by ourselves.'

'Now that I'm here,' said Beardie, 'are you going to take me to the park?'

'All right, just a little walk,' said Ted.

Ted ran down the side of the house and shouted through the open back door, 'Mum, I'm just going down as far as the park gates.'

As he walked along, he wondered what on earth he could do about Beardie.

The town pigeons followed Ted and Beardie. When they got to the park gates, they met the park pigeons who began a loud argument about who had done most for Beardie, the park or the town birds. They flitted into groups and flew at each other, then strutted about, with no bird listening to another.

'I hope they're not going to fight,' Ted said to Speckles.

'Oh no. They're enjoying a family row,' replied Speckles. 'We don't often all get together.'

Ted walked back down the road, planning what to say to Mum. Beardie followed close behind.

'You wait here by the gate,' said Ted, 'while I go and talk to Mum.'

'Oh there you are, Ted,' said Mum.

'Mum, Beardie's run away from the home,' Ted blurted.

'How do you know? Where is he?' asked Mum.

'He's outside,' said Ted. 'He found his way back to our street.'

'I suppose he wouldn't want to go back to the house with that cruel man,' said Mum.

'I think he wants to live with me,' said Ted.

'Now, Ted,' said Mum, 'how could you know what a dog wants to do?'

Ted opened his mouth to answer but he knew she wouldn't believe him. 'Please, can he live with us?' he begged.

'Now Ted, you know that's impossible. Even if we could afford to feed a dog, we couldn't shut him in all day.'

'I suppose not,' said Ted sadly.

'We'll have to ring up the dogs' home and tell them he's here. They'll come and take him back,' said Mum.

'But what do we tell Beardie?' asked Ted.

'We can't tell a dog anything,' said Mum. 'But don't worry. He'll be OK.'

Just then Beardie came bounding up the path and following behind him was Mr Appleby.

'How did you get here, boy?' said
Mr Appleby. 'Surely this isn't the dog you
rescued, Ted? They must have done a
fine job at the dogs' home. Come here,
boy. Let's have a look at you.'

Beardie went up to Mr Appleby in a
friendly way. Mr Appleby patted him
and asked Ted what was going on.

'Beardie's come back. He seems to
want to live here,' Ted told him.

'But he can't possibly stay here,' said
Mum. 'Please may we use your phone to
ring up the dogs' home? They'll be
worried, as he's run away.'

'Wait a minute,' said Mr Appleby.
'What he needs is a good home. And
I've half a mind to take him on myself.'

'Beardie live here!' exclaimed Ted. He could hardly believe his ears.

'I am getting on, and he might be a bit lively for me,' said Mr Appleby, 'but perhaps Ted could take him out for me sometimes.'

'Everyday. Any time,' Ted gabbled.

'What does your mum think of sharing a dog?'

'It might work,' she said. 'He could keep you company in the day…'

'…and sleep with us,' pleaded Ted.

'I'd pay for his food,' Mr Appleby went on. 'They do say that a dog is man's best friend.'

'He'd be my very best friend,' said Ted.

'I'll go in and phone the people at the dogs' home,' said Mr Appleby.

While Ted was waiting for Mr Appleby to come off the phone, he found a crust and threw out crumbs for the birds, who were waiting eagerly outside. Ted saw Mouse sitting on the back door step by her hole. He picked her up and put her in his pocket.

Then he went back inside and
hurried upstairs. 'What did they say?'
Ted asked.

'They want me to have a week's trial,' Mr Appleby reported. 'Warned me that Beardie would need a lot of patience and grooming, but I said I'd have help ...'

'You will,' interrupted Ted.

'I know he is a clever dog, but it's a mystery to me how he found his way to you,' Mr Appleby went on.

'It's not a mystery to me,' thought Ted.

Will Ted ever tell his friends that he can talk to animals?

Do you think the animals will go on talking to Ted?